Theodore and the Whale

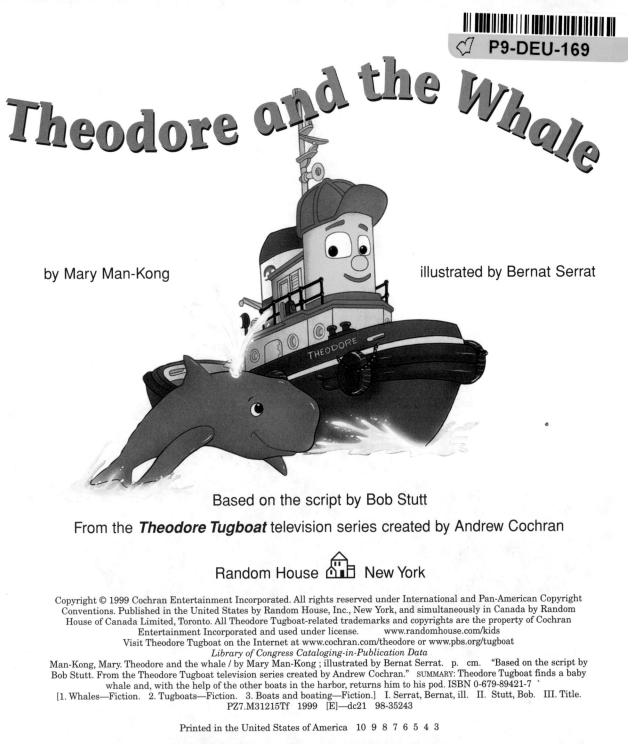

by Mary Man-Kong

illustrated by Bernat Serrat

Based on the script by Bob Stutt

From the **Theodore Tugboat** television series created by Andrew Cochran

Random House 🏠 New York

Copyright © 1999 Cochran Entertainment Incorporated. All rights reserved under International and Pan-American Copyright Conventions. Published in the United States by Random House, Inc., New York, and simultaneously in Canada by Random House of Canada Limited, Toronto. All Theodore Tugboat-related trademarks and copyrights are the property of Cochran Entertainment Incorporated and used under license.   www.randomhouse.com/kids
Visit Theodore Tugboat on the Internet at www.cochran.com/theodore or www.pbs.org/tugboat
Library of Congress Cataloging-in-Publication Data
Man-Kong, Mary. Theodore and the whale / by Mary Man-Kong ; illustrated by Bernat Serrat. p. cm. "Based on the script by Bob Stutt. From the Theodore Tugboat television series created by Andrew Cochran." SUMMARY: Theodore Tugboat finds a baby whale and, with the help of the other boats in the harbor, returns him to his pod. ISBN 0-679-89421-7
[1. Whales—Fiction. 2. Tugboats—Fiction. 3. Boats and boating—Fiction.] I. Serrat, Bernat, ill. II. Stutt, Bob. III. Title.
PZ7.M31215Tf 1999 [E]—dc21 98-35243

Printed in the United States of America 10 9 8 7 6 5 4 3

PICTUREBACK is a registered trademark of Random House, Inc.

One day after a storm, Theodore Tugboat was exploring the shoreline of The Big Harbor. He was on his way to the morning meeting at The Great Ocean Dock.

Suddenly, he heard a strange sound coming from a pile of logs.

"What is that?" Theodore asked. It sounded like crying.

Theodore floated closer.

"Something's in there!" said Theodore. "I have to help!"

Quickly, he attached his tow-rope to one of the logs and pulled. The logs began to move, and out swam—a baby whale!

"Where did *you* come from?" asked Theodore.

The young whale didn't answer. Instead, he rubbed against Theodore's hull and whistled happily.

"It's nice to meet you, too," Theodore laughed.

The young whale followed Theodore to the morning meeting.
The tugboats were surprised to see him.

"He must have gotten lost in the storm," George said.

"I wish *I* had a pet whale," Hank laughed as the whale bumped his nose against him.

"He's not a pet, Hank," said Emily. "Whales can't stay in the harbor. They need to be out in the ocean. We have to find his friends."

"I'll ask Rebecca, The Research Vessel, what to do," Theodore said. "She knows more about whales than anyone."

"He must have come into the harbor after being separated from the other whales in his pod," Rebecca said when she saw him.

"They must wonder where he is," said Theodore.

"Yes," Rebecca agreed. "I'll ask the Dispatcher to send out George to search for them."

"But what about me?" Theodore asked. "I want to go search for the other whales."

"I'm sorry, Theodore," said Rebecca. "You need to stay here with this whale until his friends are found."

"You mean I have to be a...whale-sitter?" Theodore asked. "But I'm a tugboat! I have work to do!"

"He needs you, Theodore," said Rebecca.

At first, Theodore was upset that he had to whale-sit.

But he soon forgot all that, because playing with the baby whale was so much fun!

"You must play these games with your friends," Theodore laughed.

When Theodore said the word *friends,* the little whale became sad.

"You miss them, don't you?" asked Theodore.

"Don't worry," Theodore said. "We'll find them.

"I wish you could tell me your name," said Theodore. "I know, maybe I could give you a name to use while you're here. I'll call you…Walter. Okay?"

The young whale splashed around happily.

"Come on, Walter!" called Theodore. "Let's go explore the harbor!"

That evening, Walter slept near Theodore's dock while the tugs talked quietly.

"George still hasn't returned from searching for Walter's friends," Emily whispered.

"What if we can't find them?" asked Theodore.
"I guess Walter will stay here forever," Hank said.
"Then I could look after him," said Theodore eagerly.
"And we could be together every day!"

At the tugboat meeting the next morning, Walter swam around the tugs while the Dispatcher assigned the various jobs.

"Theodore," said the Dispatcher, "your job today is to keep an eye on Walter."

"Great!" Theodore exclaimed.

Walter was so happy that he soaked the
Dispatcher with a spray of water!

All the tugboats were shocked. The
Dispatcher didn't like getting wet! But
even he had to smile at Walter.

Then Walter started squirting
everyone!

Soon all the tugs were laughing and squirting one another.
"What's going on here?" George spluttered as someone squirted
him with water.
The tugs stopped what they were doing and looked at George.

"Did you find the other whales?" asked Hank.

"Yes, I found them," George said. "They're waiting just outside the harbor. They're too big to come in."

Everyone cheered. Everyone...but Theodore.

"Well, Walter, it's time for you to go home," said Emily.

"Theodore, there's something I would like you to do," the Dispatcher said. "Theodore?"

Everyone turned to Theodore, but Theodore was...gone.

Theodore didn't know what to do. He decided to talk to Rebecca. "I thought Walter would stay forever," Theodore said.

"You know Walter can't live in a harbor," said Rebecca. "Whales grow to a tremendous size. And they like to be with other whales—just the way you like to be with other tugboats."

"But Walter was my friend," Theodore said.

Bump! Theodore felt something push up against him.

"Walter!" Theodore exclaimed. "What are you doing here?"

"He wants you to lead him out of the harbor," Emily said gently. "And the Dispatcher said it was all right."

Theodore and Walter floated toward the open ocean.
Theodore was still very sad that Walter was leaving.
Suddenly, he felt a squirt of water. It was Walter!
Theodore laughed. It made him feel a lot better.
"Good-bye," he called softly.

Theodore slowly returned to the harbor.
"Was it hard saying good-bye?" asked Hank.
"It was hard," Theodore replied. "But then I
realized I haven't lost a pet...I've gained a
friend!"